Space Dogs

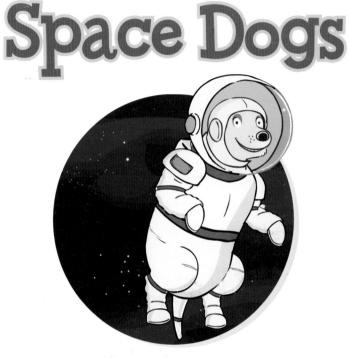

Adaptation by Jamie White

Based on a TV series teleplay

written by Ken Scarborough

Based on characters created by Susan Meddaugh

HOUGHTON MIFFLIN HARCOURT

Boston New York

For information about permission to reproduce selections from this book, write to Permissions, Houghton Mifflin Harcourt Publishing Company, 215 Park Avenue South, New York, New York 10003. Library of Congress Cataloging-in-Publication Data is on file.

Cover design by Rachel Newborn. Book design by Bill Smith Group.

ISBN 978-0-547-68119-1 hc | ISBN 978-0-547-68118-4 pb

www.hmhbooks.com
www.marthathetalkingdog.com

Manufactured in Singapore
TWP 10 9 8 7 6 5 4 3 2 1
4500343671

GREETINGS, EARTHLINGS!

I am Space Dog Martha, an alien visitor from the planet of dogs. I have come to Earth to tell you this story. And to pick up the best pizza in the galaxy. (Won't *anybody* here deliver to outer space?)

Just kidding. I'm not a space dog. (That'd be a little farfetched!) No, I'm Martha the *talking* dog.

Ever since Helen fed me her alphabet soup, I've been able to speak. And speak and speak . . .

No one's sure how or why, but the letters in the soup travel up to my brain instead of down to my stomach.

Now as long as I eat my daily bowl of alphabet soup, I can talk. To my family—Helen, baby Jake, Mom, Dad, and Skits, who only speaks Dog. To Helen's best human friend, T.D. To anyone who'll listen.

Sometimes my family wishes I didn't talk quite so much. But my speaking comes in handy. Like the time I called 911 to bust a burglar. Or when I gave T.D. an out-of-this-world idea for his class project.

It's too bad things kind of got away from him. Keep reading to find out how.

The countdown to chapter one begins now. Three . . . two . . . ONE!

SLOBBER ON NEPTUNE

Helen and T.D.'s teacher, Mrs. Clusky, asked the class to create a project about the solar system.

"Our solar system is made up of the sun and all of the planets that orbit around it," Mrs. Clusky said.

"What does *orbit* mean?" asked T.D.

"*Orbit* means 'to travel around something else,' " she explained. "The earth and the other planets orbit, or go around, the sun. Any more questions?"

T.D. raised his hand. "Ooo ooo! What kind of cheese is the moon made of?"

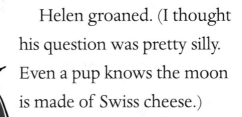

Helen groaned. (I thought his question was pretty silly. Even a pup knows the moon is made of Swiss cheese.)

On the walk home from school, Helen told T.D. her plan. "I'll build a model solar system. My basketball would make a perfect sun."

"I guess that's an OK idea," said T.D.

"Well, what's your idea?"

T.D. smiled. "Only the best class project in the history of class projects! Thanks to one of my dad's coolest inventions!"

Later that day, he showed it off to the neighborhood kids.

"The Autojet 8000!" T.D. announced.

The crowd gasped at his project—a jetpack! T.D. held its controls. With a touch of a button, he'd be launched into space.

"My dad invented it," he said. "While everyone else is stuck on Earth dreaming of space, I'll be up there taking pictures. Now to begin the launch sequence! Ten. Nine. Eight— "

"Uh, T.D.?" Helen interrupted.

"Shhh!" he said. "Not now. Seven. Six. Five. Four—"

"But T.D.," said Helen.

Smoke puffed out of the jetpack's thrusters.

"It's too late!" said T.D. "There's no turning back. Farewell, good people and dogs of Earth! Prepare to witness the best class project EVER! Three. Two. One . . ."

WHOOSH! He disappeared behind a huge cloud of smoke.

Holy cow! He really did it, I thought.

When the smoke cleared, the jetpack was gone. But T.D. was still there. He stared at the controls in his hands. The kids giggled.

"I was trying to tell you," said Helen. "You forgot to buckle up."

"Oops."

After his failed launch, T.D. sulked as Helen
started her own project. She searched for a
basketball in the garage.

"Aha!" she said, holding it up. "This will be
the sun for my solar system."

*Or a tasty second course to this tennis ball I'm
chewing*, I thought. *Mmm.*

"Martha!" said Helen. "You're getting
slobber all over Neptune!"

"Neptune? Looks like a ball to me," I said.

"For my project, each ball is a planet," said Helen. "A planet is a large round object in space that orbits a star. Our planet, Earth, orbits the sun. See?"

Helen revolved the tennis ball around the basketball. "When you put all of the planets together, it's called the solar system."

"You make the solar system look so chewable," I said, going in for another bite.

"Sorry, Martha. No dog drool on my planets."

T.D. sighed loudly.

"What's the matter, T.D.?" asked Helen.

"I wish *I* lived on another planet. One where I didn't have to do class projects. Without my jetpack, I have no idea what to do." He hid his face in his hands.

"You'll think of something," said Helen. "Right now, I need to find a Jupiter."

Helen spotted a green ball in a box on a high shelf. "Perfect!" she said, moving a ladder to reach it.

But the ladder knocked the box to the ground. *Bang!* What spilled out of it was about to make T.D.'s day.

CHUCK'S BAD LUCK

"Cool!" said T.D. "What are those?"

"Just my dad's old comics," Helen said.

T.D. held one up. *"The Outer Space Chronicles of Chuck Nebula,"* he read. "Hey, he looks like me!"

T.D. looked as much like Chuck Nebula as I did. As in *not at all.*

"Can I borrow these?" he asked. "Maybe they'll help me think of an idea for my project."

"Sure," said Helen.

While T.D. left with the comics, my jaws landed on Jupiter. *Chomp!*

"Martha!" Helen scolded.

"I can't help it," I said. Dogs chew. It's what we do.

Two days later, Helen worked on her model solar system in the kitchen. She was talking to me. But all I heard was blah, blah, blah. How could I listen near so much chewy goodness? Couldn't she spare Saturn? A munch of Mars?

"Earth to Martha," said Helen.

"Sorry. You said the sun is a star?" I asked.

"That's right."

"But wait. The sun is way bigger and brighter than a star is. Stars are tiny things that only come out at night."

"Stars look small because they're far away, but actually they're big balls of burning gas, like the sun," said Helen. "The sun is a star that's close to us, so it looks bigger."

We looked at the sun out the window.

Suddenly, it was eclipsed by T.D.'s big head!

"AGGGH!" Helen and I screamed.

T.D. waved a comic book wildly.

His mouth was moving, but we couldn't hear what he was saying.

"What's T.D. doing here?" I asked.

Helen sighed. "He probably spent all weekend reading comic books and still has no idea what to do for his project."

She opened the window and T.D. fell in headfirst. "Whoa!"

He held up the comic. "I spent all weekend reading comic books and still have NO idea what to do for my project!"

"Mmm-hmm," said Helen.

"But that's the least of my problems." T.D. opened to a page. "Look! Chuck is finally able to fend off the evil Omega Squad androids. But they blow up his spaceship. So he uses his escape pod and ends up on a deserted planet!"

"And?" said Helen.

"That's the problem. I DON'T KNOW!" T.D. turned to a page with a giant question mark. "To be continued! I can't stand 'To be continueds'!"

That's why it's too bad this chapter ends here.

To be continued . . . (Sorry, T.D.)

WHEN SPACE CATS ATTACK

"Where's the last comic book in the series?" T.D. asked. "I'll go *crazy* if I don't find out how it ends!"

Helen shrugged. "I only saw the comics that were in the box."

Just then, Dad walked in.

"Dad!" said Helen. "We found your favorite comic!"

His face lit up. *"Pinky the Pony?"*

"Um," said Helen, "guess again."

T.D. showed him the comic book.

"The Outer Space Chronicles!" Dad
exclaimed. "This is the one where Chuck
battles the Omega Squad androids and . . ."

"Commander Zylon uses his freeze ray to
turn Chuck into a block of ice!" said T.D.

Dad did his best block of ice imitation.
"You'll . . . never . . . get . . . away . . . with . . .
this . . . Zylon!" he said in a robotic voice.

Helen and I looked at each other. Male humans can be so strange.

"I need to find the next issue to see what happens," said T.D.

Dad sighed. "I hate to tell you this, but Baltimore Comics went out of business after that issue."

"You mean this is the *last one?*" T.D. cried. "There's *no ending?*"

"That's right. I was so depressed when I found out. I didn't get over that for years." Dad opened the fridge and poured himself a glass of juice. "Somehow, I managed to forget it. Until now."

He downed his OJ and left looking sadder than a hound dog.

"A whole *lifetime?*" said T.D. "It was bad enough having to wonder about Chuck Nebula all morning."

"Why don't you draw the last comic?" I suggested. "That could be your school project—finishing up the story once and for all."

T.D. smiled. "Dogs have the best ideas!"

Unfortunately for dogs everywhere, Skits chose this moment to burst in chasing his tail. He crossed the kitchen like a furry tornado.

"Sometimes," T.D. corrected himself.

We went to Helen's room to get started. She worked at her desk. Sprawled out on the floor, T.D. drew his comic as I looked on.

"Here we go," he said. "When we last saw Chuck Nebula, he was stranded on a deserted planet."

"Maybe the planet isn't really deserted," I said. "In fact, there's a dog."

T.D. added a snazzy space dog. She looked just like me. Space Dog Martha.

"Actually, there are lots of dogs," I added. "It's a planet ruled by dogs. The planet of dogs!"

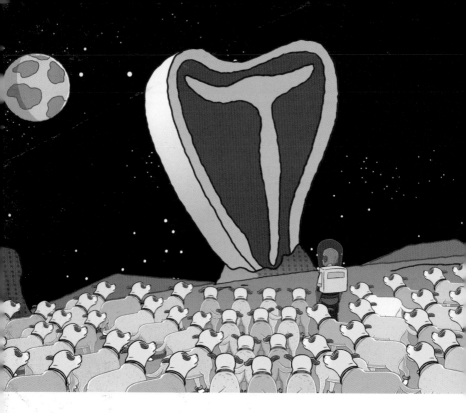

Now lots of Marthas appeared.

"And the dogs are happy because they've
just discovered the secret of the universe,"
I said.

At my suggestion, T.D. drew the secret—a
steak as big as the moon. Yum!

"The end," I said.

"No," said T.D., erasing the steak. "The dogs are upset. Because they're under attack by evil space cats hurling radioactive hairballs!"

He drew a new scene . . .

SOCKING IT TO SPACE PIRATES

"But help was on the way!" Helen cried.

T.D. and I jumped. How long had she been reading over our shoulders?

"What?" she said. "I wanted to help."

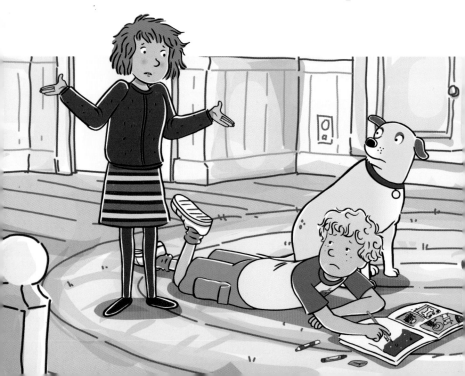

Back in T.D.'s comic, evil cats were lapping up the escape pod's fuel when out of nowhere, a giant laundry basket sped toward them.

"A laundry basket?" asked Helen.

"Sure," said T.D. "I always pretend our laundry basket is a spaceship."

One day, I'll return all of the socks to the good people of Earth.

BUT THEN ... SPACE PIRATES APPEAR! THEY'VE COME TO STEAL THE SOCKS AND TURN THEM INTO AN EVIL ARMY OF SOCK PUPPETS.

BUT THEIR VACUUM WAS TOO STRONG...

"What's with the vacuum?" asked Helen.

"I definitely heard Mrs. Clusky say something about the giant vacuum of space," said T.D.

The next morning, T.D. read his comic to the class.

"And they all lived happily ever after, making sure that no socks were used for evil purposes."

"Well," said Mrs. Clusky, "I didn't understand the ending. But you did use a lot of space vocabulary. Still, I wish you'd been more realistic. Things like that don't really happen in space."

"Look!" shouted a girl, pointing to the window. "Something's falling from the sky!"

The class rushed over to see a
strange object hurtling toward them.
WHOOOOOOOOSH!

"What is it?" someone asked.

"It's . . . it's . . ." T.D. stammered.

CRASH! The school shook as the mystery
object landed.

"A *jetpack?*" Mrs. Clusky laughed. "Well, I
guess there are some things in space we don't
know much about. All right, T.D. B-plus!"

T.D. beamed a Jupiter-size smile.

He wasn't the only one happy about his comic. Dad read it before bed. *"Ka-pow! Woo! Boom!"* he shouted. "Take that, space pirates!

"This is great! It finally has an ending." Dad laughed. "Watch out! *POW!*"

It was pretty great. I only wished Space Dog Martha's adventure hadn't come to an end. I didn't know then that I'd be going to the planet of dogs the very next day . . .

PLANET MARTHA

It was that time of day. Time to wait by the fridge before Helen grabbed her afterschool snack.

I watched her open the fridge door. "Can I have a snack too?" I begged.

"We've had this discussion," said Helen, taking out two yogurts. "Too much mooching makes too much Martha."

"And the problem with that is . . .?" I asked.

She handed a yogurt to T.D., sitting at the table. "Do you guys have this discussion every day?" he asked.

"Every *day*?" Helen exclaimed. "Every time I open the refrigerator!"

"If I could get it myself, I'd never ask," I said. "But the sad fact of this world is that if you want the good stuff, you need hands."

"She's got a point,"
T.D. agreed.

"Just another way dogs are discriminated against," I said. "I really wanted to hear your report about the planet of dogs yesterday, but that mean janitor never lets me into the school."

"I'm sorry," said Helen.

I perked up. "Sorry enough to give me a snack?"

"Uh, no."

"You can take my comic if that would make you feel better," said T.D.

Comics are *not* tasty snacks. (Believe me, I've tried them.) But I supposed I could look at the pictures. I took it to my chair and got comfy.

The planet of dogs, I thought dreamily. *Wouldn't it be great to live there?* I yawned and rested my head on T.D.'s comic.

The next thing I knew, an alarm was going off.

BEEP. BEEP. BEEP . . .

"Space Dog Martha, time to wake up," said a voice.

I opened my eyes and looked around. I was
in a strange land of rocks and craters. Holy
space pajamas! I knew where I was—*the planet
of dogs!* Planet Martha. And according to the
symbols flashing in the air,
I was late for school.
Do you know
the best part about
Planet Martha?
Space dogs
don't need
hands! They shoot

powerful rays out of their ears to pick things up. Check this out. Just by pointing my ears at my backpack, I could put it on.

Cool, huh?

I ran to school. It was my turn to give a report in front of the class.

I found a room full of Marthas smiling back at me.

"My report is on the universe," I said. "The universe is everything. It's space itself

and everything in space, like planets, stars, and asteroids. Asteroids are big rocks in space that are smaller than planets but bigger than a spaceship."

Stars and planets floated across the viewscreen.

"One planet in the universe is called Earth. There's something strange about Earth. It has only one moon!"

The Marthas gasped.

"Recently, some astronauts visited us from Earth. They left behind this book, *The Outer Space Chronicles of Chuck Nebula*. It's about a very important person on Earth named Chuck Nebula. He might even be king of the Earth people."

"He's dreamy," said a Martha in the audience.

"Unfortunately," I said, "we don't know what happened to Chuck Nebula. There's no ending to the story. It just says, 'To be continued.' And that's my report on the universe. The end."

The Marthas cheered.

"If there's one thing I hate," said Teacher Martha, "it's stories that end with 'To be continued.' If you want extra credit, you could fly to Earth and find out what happened to the Earthling king Chuck Nebula."

Great idea! Naturally. (She was a Martha, after all.)

ALIEN INVASION!

Where on Earth was Chuck Nebula? I'd been circling the planet for hours in my spaceship, but there was no sign of him.

"Wait. What's this?" My camera zoomed in on a Yorkie walking along a sidewalk. Nearby, a mean-looking bald man hid in the bushes. He was holding a net.

"This way, little poochie," he said.

I pressed a button on my control panel to reveal his identity. "LOUIE KABLOOIE. BAD EARTHLING," I read. "Oh, no!"

He threw his net over the dog. "Gotcha!"

"That poor creature!" I said. "Computer, fix coordinates. We're going in!"

My spaceship landed in a place called Wagstaff City, USA. I left my ship on City Hall's lawn and ran past some Earthlings.

"Hang on, little guy!" I called. "I'm on my way."

An old woman gasped. "Did you see that? A space dog just got out of that giant bone! It's an *ALIEN INVASION!*"

What's an invasion? I wondered. But this was no time for vocabulary questions.

Outside a pet shop, Louie Kablooie tied the little dog to a parking meter. He hid her

collar in his pocket. "Not a yap out of you," he snarled. "Or else."

The dog whimpered as Kablooie walked into the store.

"Heh, heh," he snickered. "I'm going to make a bundle off that pedigreed pooch."

From around a corner, I watched Kablooie disappear into the shop to sell that dog. *Well, not if I can help it, mister!* I pointed my ears at the dog's rope and untied it.

"Don't worry, little friend. We're getting you out of here," I said. "That guy is not humane."

Arf, arf!

"Yes, he *is* human. But he's not humane," I said. "*Humane* means 'kind.' And that guy is not being humane to you. In fact, what he's doing is inhumane!"

Arf!

"Nice to meet you, Daisy," I said. "I'm—"

"Hey!" someone yelled. "What are you doing?"

Yikes! It was Louie Kablooie.

"RUN!" I cried.

Daisy and I took off down the street with the bad guy on our tails. We ducked into an alley to lose him.

"Uh-oh," I said, looking around. "Dead end."

He came around the corner. "Gotcha!"

"That's what you think, you inhumane meanie-pants!" I said. "Follow me, Daisy!"

Using my super space paws, I dug an escape tunnel before Kablooie could take another step.

"Down we go!" I cried. Daisy and I jumped in.

"Come back here!" he shouted into the hole.

But we were already nearing the end of the tunnel. And even better, I smelled steak.

NO DOGS ALLOWED

What luck! Daisy and I had ended up in front of a fancy restaurant.

"All that digging works up an appetite," I said. "Let's eat!"

I stepped inside. Daisy hesitated by the door. It was like she'd never dined out before. "Well?" I said. "Come in!"

We sat at a table. A man in a suit came to greet us.

"Ah! Hello, my good man," I said. "We'll start with two steaks. Rare!"

The man scowled at us.

"What, you don't serve steaks?" I asked.

"No. We don't serve *dogs!*" he shouted, chasing us out. Daisy and I were back on the street. We didn't even get doggy bags.

"Well!" I said. "I have some serious objections to how this planet is run. When I find Chuck Nebula, I'm going to give him a piece of my mind!"

Arf!

"You say you've never heard of Chuck Nebula? Hmm. For a king, he's not very well known."

Meanwhile, at the mayor's office, a certain Mrs. Parkington was making sure I was well known. She was the old woman who'd seen me land. Leading a group of citizens, she told the mayor I was invading Earth.

"Invasion?" the mayor asked. "What are you talking about?"

"An invasion is when a large group goes to a place and tries to take it over," said Mrs. Parkington. "And I tell you, alien dogs are invading our world and trying to take it over!"

It was difficult for the mayor to deny this with my spaceship parked on her lawn.

"That's no ordinary giant rocket-powered bone outside," said Mrs. Parkington. "That's an alien space bone if I ever saw one!"

The others agreed.

"And the creature that got out of it is not from this world. It's an EXTRATERRESTRIAL!"

"An extraterrestrial?" said the mayor. "Interesting. Uh, just let me check something with my secretary."

She hurried out of her office.

"I hope she's planning to do something quickly," huffed Mrs. Parkington.

Suddenly, they heard a loud *SCREECH* as the mayor's car sped past the window. Yup. The mayor was doing something quickly, all right—fleeing town faster than I flee a bath.

Daisy and I walked down the street, searching for Chuck Nebula. We didn't find him. But we did see Louie Kablooie talking with a hot dog vendor.

"Hey, did you see that?" Kablooie asked him. "Around the corner? It's a parade!"

The hot dog guy took off to look for the parade. Then Kablooie took off with his weenie cart.

"I have to do something about this!" I said. As Kablooie tried sneaking away, I pointed my ears at him. *Zap!* I lifted him into the air and kept him there.

"Whoa! What's going on?" he hollered as I guided him to me. "What's happening?"

"I'll tell you what's happening," I said, dropping him to the ground. "You are getting a lesson in manners. First you were not humane to Daisy. Then you tried to steal a weenie cart. Now stop it and get out of here!"

I lifted him to his feet and released him from my hold. That big bully ran off crying like a baby.

"And be more honest!" I called after him. "Like dogs."

Daisy thanked me with an *Arf!*.

"No problem. All in a day's work."

Just then, someone behind us shouted, "There they are!"

Daisy and I turned to see the man from the restaurant pointing at us. He was with a guy holding two leashes and a cage.

A moment later, Daisy and I were locked behind bars. Wouldn't you know it. Even space dogs can end up in the shelter.

WANTED: SPACE MUTT

"What is this?" I asked from my cage. "They throw you in the shelter for nothing?"

I was doing time with Daisy, a dachshund, and a hardened old boxer.

Woof! barked the boxer.

"Yes, I have no tags," I replied. "But I'm not from your world. I'm a space dog."

Woof!

"Really, I am!" I walked out of my cage to face him. "Why don't you believe me?"

His jaw dropped. *Woof?!*

"How did I get out?" I said. "I opened the cage. Like this."

I raised my ears. *Zap!* Daisy's door swung open. "Can't you do that?" I asked them.

They tried. But it was no use.

"Oh, well," I said. "No problem."

Zap! Zap! I opened the other two cages and the dogs were free. Now I had to get back to finding Chuck Nebula.

"Right after a snack," I said, spotting a fridge.

The others watched hopefully as I raised my ears. With a *zap*, I opened the fridge door.

"Wow! Bread, bologna, pickles, ketchup, and mustard," I said, guiding everything out. "I know what to make with this."

I dumped all the food into one sloppy pile. "A delicious mess! Dinner, gang!"

My new friends joined me at the feast. But while we were chewing, trouble was brewing. Although I didn't know it, people all over town were looking for me!

"The mayor's office has offered a reward for the alien seen leaving this spacecraft," said the TV announcer.

If I had known that Earthlings were after me, I would have gone home then and there. Instead, the dogs and I went for a walk. As we strolled through town, they asked me lots of questions.

"Where am I from?" I said. "I'm an extraterrestrial."

Yap!

"An extraterrestrial is someone from space. You know, someone who isn't from Earth. I'm from Planet Martha. On my planet, dogs rule."

Hiding in a doorway, Louie Kablooie hung on my every word. "I knew it! That dog is the alien! I'm about to get a reward for capturing that stinking space mutt!"

He stepped in front of me. "Did I hear you say you're a talking dog from space?"

"Yes. And you're that bad guy," I said.

"But I've changed my ways," Kablooie said sweetly. "Thanks to you. Come with me."

"Where are you going?"

"Well, I'm not really supposed to tell, but we're planning a little welcome-to-Earth party," he said. "It's at the mayor's office."

A party? For me? How nice! I thought.

"Did someone say my name?" a voice asked. The mayor, driving a moving truck, was stopped next to us.

"Ms. Mayor?" said Kablooie.

"Yes, I was attempting to discover the facts about the aliens using this, er, moving truck."

Hmm. The only thing the mayor looks like she's trying to discover is a new address, I thought.

"Well, it's just one alien," said Kablooie. "And I caught her. It's this dog!"

"Good work!" said the mayor. She whistled to a policewoman. "Officer? Please arrest that alien."

I guessed this meant my party was off.

BETTER THAN CHEESE SNOODLES

The mayor ordered the policewoman to let her know when I was locked up. "I'll be, uh, continuing my investigations in the next town," she said.

Then—*VROOOM!*—the mayor sped away.

"Wait a minute," I said.

I pointed my ears at her truck. *Zap!* I lifted it into the air and flew it back to me. It stayed there, hovering.

"Uh-oh," said Kablooie, slinking away.

"Why should I be locked up?" I asked the mayor.

"Because we don't know anything about you," she said. "You could be dangerous."

"But I come in peace! I'd like to speak to Chuck Nebula about some improvements to your planet."

"Chuck *who?*" asked the mayor.

Geesh. A mayor should really know the name of her king, I thought.

Little did I know that while we were talking, Kablooie was up to his old tricks. "LOOK!" he shouted. "THE SPACE DOG HAS THE MAYOR TRAPPED!"

Across the street, Mrs. Parkington and her group took notice. "Did you hear that?" she asked them. "The alien! That way!"

Meanwhile, the mayor had just told me some shocking news.

"So you're saying Chuck Nebula is only in comic books?" I said. "This is *not* going to be good for my extra credit report."

"Do you mind putting my truck down now?" she asked.

"GET HER!" Mrs. Parkington shouted from behind me. "GET THE ALIEN!"

Uh-oh. I dropped the truck and turned to face the angry crowd. This did not look good.

"I come in peace! I'm not an invader!" I cried, backing into a doorway. "Really! REALLY!"

They were closing in on me. I was a goner!
I just wanted to go home.

"There's no place like space," I said,
squeezing my eyes shut. "There's no place like
space. There's no place like—AGH!"

My eyes flew open. I looked around.

I was back in my chair with T.D.'s comic in
front of me. Whoa. What a dream! It seemed
so real.

*Maybe being a space
dog isn't so great after
all,* I thought.
*Although it was
nice to not need
hands. Hmm. I
wonder . . .*

In the kitchen, I pointed my ears at the fridge and concentrated. *Open . . . Open . . . Open . . .*

Gah! My ears drooped. Why can't things be like in dreams?

"Trying to make the refrigerator door open by itself?" asked Helen.

"Something like that."

"Well, you've been a good girl today. I suppose one snack wouldn't hurt." Helen threw me a treat.

"My favorite," I said, gobbling it up. "You know what? Even though I've learned a lot about space over the past few days, there are some pretty nice things about Earth."

"Cheese Snoodles? Is that your favorite thing about Earth?"

"No," I said. *"You're* my favorite thing."

"Aww!" Helen hugged me.

"But," I said, eyeing another treat, "Cheese Snoodles are a close second."

MARTHA SUPREMO

T.D.'s and Helen's class projects are done. But you know what? I still dream about exploring our solar system.

Maybe one day I'll be Astronaut Martha and travel around in space. Or Astronomer Martha, a scientist who studies stars. But last night, I found an easier way to see space.

Helen and I had gone for a walk. We almost stumbled over T.D. lying on his lawn and looking up at the sky.

"What are you doing?" asked Helen.

"Stargazing," he replied. "I'm thinking about what it would be like to be out there in space."

We joined him.

"I love looking for constellations," said Helen.

"Consta-what?" I asked.

"A constellation is a group of stars. When you see them from far away, you can imagine they make a picture," she said, pointing. "See Equuleus? It's a constellation that might look a little like a horse."

"My favorite constellations are Draco, the dragon, and Ursa Major, the big bear," said T.D. "Hey! I think I just discovered a new constellation."

He drew in the air with his finger to show
me how the stars connected. "This star to that
star . . . and there's the nose, and . . ."

The constellation looked a little like someone I knew.

"It looks like you, Martha!" said T.D. "We should call it Martha Supremo!"

Now I'll always be in space, I thought happily.

"I like it," I said.

GLOSSARY

How many words do you remember from the story?

asteroid: a big rock in space that is smaller than a planet but bigger than a house.

astronaut: a person who travels around in space. Some famous astronauts are John Glenn, Neil Armstrong, and Sally Ride.

astronomer: a scientist who learns about stars.

constellation: a group of stars that when seen from far away make a picture.

extraterrestrial: a creature not from this world.

humane: kind.

invasion: the act of a bunch of people or animals going to a place and trying to take it over.

orbit: to travel around something else. The Earth and other planets orbit, or go around, the sun.

planet: a large, round object in space that orbits around a star.

solar system: the sun and all the planets that orbit around it.

star: a big ball of burning gas in space.

universe: all the planets, all the stars, everything in space, and space itself.

The Outer Space Chronicles, Starring YOU!

Imagine being an astronaut on a mission with Chuck Nebula and Space Dog Martha. Create a comic book about your adventure.

Here's how:

1 Write your story.

2 Practice drawing your characters. Don't forget their costumes!

3 Draw borders for each of your comic book panels. Panels are usually read in a Z pattern, so readers follow the action from left to right, diagonally left, and then right.

4 Add speech bubbles, sound words, and other text. Make sure to leave room for the art.

Woof!

CRASH!

5 Sketch your drawings.

6 Trace the final sketches with ink. When the ink dries, erase your pencil lines.

7 Color the images with markers.

8 When you're done, you can take your comic to a copy shop to have it printed.

T.D. can't stand stories that end with "To be continued." Using the vocabulary words, create a story or comic for one these cliffhangers:

The evil sock puppet army has invaded Planet Martha. What will Space Dog Martha do?

For extra credit on her latest report, Space Dog Martha must visit a school on Earth. *Knock-knock!* She's at your classroom door.

Chuck Nebula's escape pod is dodging asteroids when he discovers it's nearly out of milk! Can he reach a planet of cows to refuel before it's too late?